MW00890714

FIRST DAY of GROOT!

Written by Brendan Deneen
Pictures by Cale Atkinson

Los Angeles
New York

Wake up, let's go,
it's the *First Day of Groot!*
Rocket's ready—
it's time to scoot.

Breakfast is the greatest
meal of the day.
It gives you the strength
to run and play.

Brush your teeth.

And comb your hair.

Catch your ride
with time to spare!

You'll find adventure
at every turn.
Now come on, quick—
it's time to learn!

Learning to share is lesson number one.

**Friends help count numbers
like 1, 2, and 3 . . .**

**And letters that spell
G-R-O-O-T.**

We're not done yet—
there's so much to do!
After all, it's only lesson
number two.

It's time for lunch,
and look who's here!
Friends come together
from far and near.

But when out of the blue,
Thanos attacks . . .

The heroes join forces and then fight back!

Don't forget teamwork;
it's lesson number three.
Let's work together
like a super family!

Now that the day
is almost done . . .
Oh, wait! Galactic villains
on the run!

It's the final lesson;
let's learn a new song.
Turn up the music,
and let's all sing along!

The first day of GROOT
was the best first day yet . . .

Filled with lessons and fun
that we'll never forget.

Printed in Malaysia

First Edition, July 2019   10 9 8 7 6 5 4 3 2 1

ISBN: 978-1-368-00069-7

FAC-029191-19095

Library of Congress Control Number: 2018952775

Reinforced binding